Puss in Boots

by Lisa Findlay
illustrated by Tim Bowers

Random House 🏠 New York

Once upon a time,
there was a cat named Puss.
He lived with the old miller
and his three sons.
Puss would hide in the mill.
If a rat came to eat the grain,
Puss would pounce!

Then the miller died.

The oldest son took the mill.

The second son took the donkey.

"There is nothing left for me!"

said the youngest son.

"You can have the cat,"

his brothers said.

The youngest son's name was Tom.

Tom had no money

to feed a cat.

He planned to leave Puss
alone in the woods.
Puss was scared.

"I can make you rich,"

Puss said to Tom.

Tom didn't know Puss could talk.

He thought a talking cat

must be very clever.

Puss asked for a sack.

He asked for a pair of boots.

Tom gave him both things.

Puss filled the sack
with carrots.

He hid behind a rock.

Some rabbits came to eat.

Puss snatched them up

in his sack!

Puss brought the rabbits
to the king's castle.
"A present from my master,"
Puss said.
The king rubbed his stomach.
He loved rabbit stew.

"What is your master's
name?" the princess asked.
Puss told a fib.
"Lord Carabas," he said.

Puss brought a present
to the castle every week.

He brought grain from the mill.

He brought fish from the river.

He brought flowers
from the field.

One day, Puss saw
the royal carriage
coming down the road.
He had an idea.

He told Tom to go swimming

in the river.

"Now?" Tom asked.

"Now!" Puss said.

Tom stripped off his clothes.

He jumped into the river.

Puss looked down the road.
The king's carriage
was getting closer!
He hid Tom's clothes
under a rock.

Puss ran into the road.

"Help!

Lord Carabas is drowning!"

he cried.

The carriage driver fished
Tom out of the river.

Tom hid behind a bush.
"Bandits stole
my master's clothes,"
said Puss.

The king remembered the gifts

from Lord Carabas.

"Bring this man

a fine new suit," he said.

Lord Carabas got

into the carriage

with the king and the princess.

Puss saw some people
down the road.
He had another idea.
He ran ahead.

The people were picking apples.

They looked hungry.

"Why don't you eat the apples?"

Puss asked.

"We give all our apples

to a bad ogre,"

a man said.

The ogre could turn

into a dragon.

Puss made a deal
with the people.

They would tell the king
that the orchard belonged
to Lord Carabas.
Puss would get rid
of the ogre.

Puss ran on.

His boots helped him

run fast.

Puss found some people

milking cows.

They looked thirsty.

"Why don't you drink the milk?"

Puss asked.

"We give all our milk

to a scary ogre,"

a woman said.

The ogre could turn into a tiger.

Puss made a deal with
these people, too.
They would tell the king
that the cows belonged
to Lord Carabas.

Puss would get rid
of the ogre.
"It's a deal!"
said the people.

"Moo," said the cows.

Puss ran on.

Puss soon came
to the ogre's castle.
He went inside.

The ogre sat on a golden throne.

He drank from a silver cup.

He picked his nose.

He scratched his bottom.

The ogre saw Puss.

He wanted to eat

Puss for dinner.

The ogre tried to

grab the cat.

But he was too slow.

Puss jumped onto the table.

The ogre turned into a lion.

Puss was shaking in his boots.

But Puss had an idea.

"I bet you can't turn

into a rhino," he said.

The ogre became a rhino.

"A bear," Puss said.

The ogre became a bear.

"A dog," Puss said.

The ogre became a dog.

39

"I'll bet you can't turn
into a mouse," said Puss.
The ogre became a mouse.
Pounce!

Puss ate the mouse
in one bite.

Puss went outside.

The royal carriage drove up.

"Welcome to the castle

of Lord Carabas!"

he said.

The king liked
the orchard and cows.

The princess liked the castle.

She loved Lord Carabas.

He loved her, too.

They were married
the very next day.

The king brought the cake.

The apple pickers

brought apple cider.

The milkmaids brought ice cream.

Puss brought himself.

The ogre was gone,

and everyone had

enough to eat and drink.

Lord and Lady Carabas
were very happy.
She called him Tom.
He called her Jenny.

Puss gave the sack

back to Tom.

But to this day,

he still wears his boots.

For Liam
—L.F.

To my friend Gary Wilson,
who introduced me to my lady
—T.B.

Visit us on the Web!
StepIntoReading.com
rhcbooks.com

Educators and librarians, for a variety of teaching tools, visit us at RHTeachersLibrarians.com

Library of Congress Cataloging-in-Publication Data
Findlay, Lisa.
Puss in Boots / by Lisa Findlay ; illustrated by Tim Bowers.
    p. cm. "A Step 3 book."
ISBN 978-0-375-84671-7 (trade pbk.) — ISBN 978-0-375-94671-4 (lib. bdg.)
Summary: A simple retelling of the tale about the clever cat, who helps his poor master win fame, fortune, and the hand of a beautiful princess.
[1. Fairy tales. 2. Folklore—France.] I. Bowers, Tim, ill. II. Title.
PZ8.F4878Pu 2008 [E]—dc22 2006101412

Printed in the United States of America
17 16 15 14 13 12 11 10 9 8 7 6 5

This book has been officially leveled by using the F&P Text Level Gradient™ Leveling System.

Dear Parents:

Congratulations! Your child is taking the first steps on an exciting journey. The destination? Independent reading!

STEP INTO READING® will help your child get there. The program offers five steps to reading success. Each step includes fun stories and colorful art or photographs. In addition to original fiction and books with favorite characters, there are Step into Reading Non-Fiction Readers, Phonics Readers and Boxed Sets, Sticker Readers, and Comic Readers—a complete literacy program with something to interest every child.

Learning to Read, Step by Step!

Ready to Read   Preschool–Kindergarten
• big type and easy words • rhyme and rhythm • picture clues
For children who know the alphabet and are eager to begin reading.

Reading with Help   Preschool–Grade 1
• basic vocabulary • short sentences • simple stories
For children who recognize familiar words and sound out new words with help.

Reading on Your Own   Grades 1–3
• engaging characters • easy-to-follow plots • popular topics
For children who are ready to read on their own.

Reading Paragraphs   Grades 2–3
• challenging vocabulary • short paragraphs • exciting stories
For newly independent readers who read simple sentences with confidence.

Ready for Chapters   Grades 2–4
• chapters • longer paragraphs • full-color art
For children who want to take the plunge into chapter books but still like colorful pictures.

STEP INTO READING® is designed to give every child a successful reading experience. The grade levels are only guides; children will progress through the steps at their own speed, developing confidence in their reading. The F&P Text Level on the back cover serves as another tool to help you choose the right book for your child.

Remember, a lifetime love of reading starts with a single step!